# I Know My Grandma Loves Me

WRITTEN BY KATHLEEN WARD
ILLUSTRATED BY ROSEMARY ELLIS

PEANUT
BUTTER
PRESS

Text copyright ©2012 by Kathleen Ward
Illustrations copyright ©2012 by Rosemary Ellis

Peanut Butter Press
9-1060 Dakota Street
Winnipeg, MB R2N 1P2
www.peanutbutterpress.ca

The artwork in this book was rendered in watercolour, ink and acrylic.
The text is set in Lehn 242.

Book design by Rosemary Ellis

Printed and bound in Canada by Friesens Corporation ✤
The binding of this hardcover edition is sewn.

Library and Archives Canada Cataloguing in Publication

Ward, Kathleen, 1973-
I know my grandma loves me / written by Kathleen
Ward ; illustrated by Rosemary Ellis.

ISBN 978-0-9865329-6-2

I. Ellis, Rosemary, 1989-  II. Title.

PS8645.A734I56 2012          jC813'.6          C2012-907335-0

I know my grandma loves me
when she looks at me
and her eyes light up
like stars twinkling in the night.

I know my grandma loves me when I curl up in her lap
and she reads me the book I love best
over and over and over again,
as though it's the first time
she has ever read that book.

I know my grandma loves me when we go for walks
and she takes really little steps like me,
so I can keep up.

I know my grandma loves me when it's the kind of cold outside that makes your teeth chatttter, your eyelashes stick together, your nose run like a leaky tap, and still she piles on layer after layer of warm clothing, just to go sledding with me!

I know my grandma loves me
when tears roll down my cheeks
and she holds out her arms
to wrap me up tight and keep me close,
so she can hear every word I need to say.

I know my grandma loves me when music fills the room
and she stops whatever she's doing
to stomp,
twist,
twirl and jump—
dancing just like me.

I know my grandma loves me

when it's springtime

and she takes me puddle jumping

in my bright yellow boots,

knowing she might get wet.

I know my grandma loves me
when it's hot and sunny
and she patiently covers me
from head to toe with sunscreen—
even if I'm being
a squiggly,
wiggly
worm.

I know my grandma loves me
when she pushes me on the swing
and I hear her giggle and laugh as I sing,
"Again, again... Again, again... Again, again!"

I know my grandma loves me
when I drum on her pots and pans
and she grabs a spoon
        and bangs on the pots with me
    like she's playing in a rock band!

I know my grandma loves me
when I spill my crayons all over the floor and she says,
    "Look at the beautiful rainbow you made."

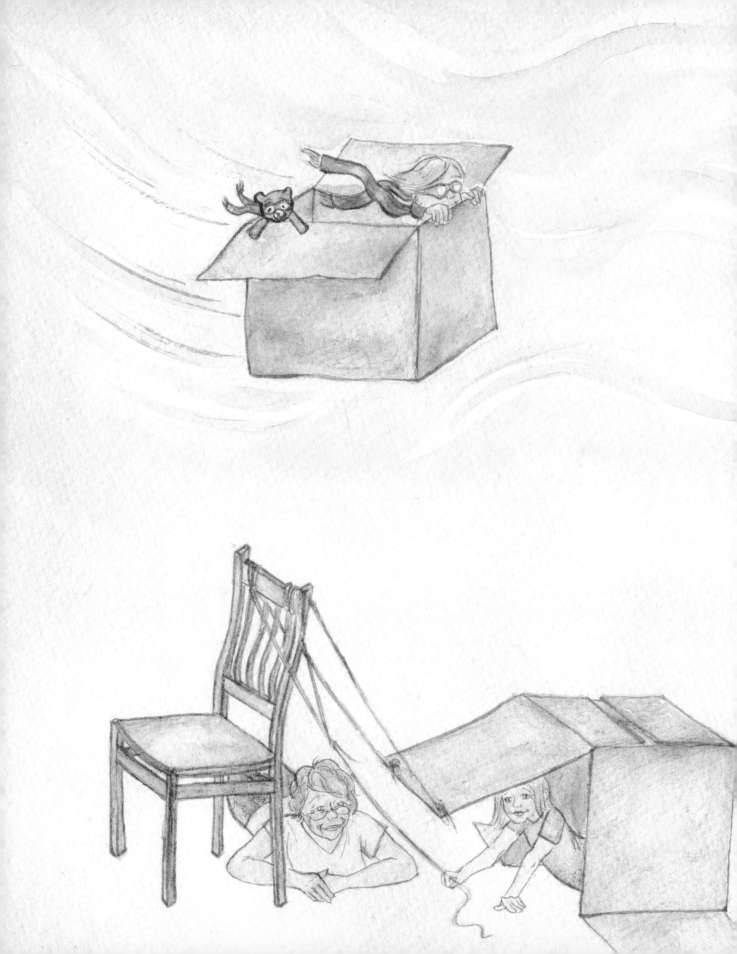

I know my grandma loves me
when she whispers,
"I have a wonderful surprise,"
and it's not a fancy present
but a big, empty box that becomes
an airplane, a fort, a climbing structure
and a blank canvas to draw on
all day long.

I know my grandma loves me when I set up my very own kitchen—
chopping carrots, broccoli and potatoes to make soup for my doll
and she quietly passes me the special spices that make my nose tingle
and my mouth water

when she makes soup for me.

I know my grandma loves me when she can't stop laughing
at the silly faces I make,
especially if she's the only one watching.

I know my grandma loves me
when she reaches into our picnic basket
and out comes juicy watermelon, ripe strawberries,
crunchy pickles, rainbow lollipops...
and my eyes open wider and wider
as I realize that we're going to
m u n c h   m u n c h   m u n c h
until our tummies are full,
just like the caterpillar we love
in the story we've shared
since I was born.

I know my grandma loves me when we're having a tea party and she surprises me with apple juice that we sip daintily as we nibble on freshly baked cookies.

I know my grandma loves me
when she makes me a birthday cake
and it's in the shape
of what I love most
right now—
        a butterfly.

I know my grandma loves me when we go to the zoo
and we pretend to be all the different animals,

from R-R-Roaring lions and scr e-e-e-e-e-ching monkeys

to tiny, croaking frogs.

I know my grandma loves me
when I walk in the door and she scoops me up,
swinging me around and around
until she catches me in a giant hug,
not caring that my boots are dripping with mud.

I know my grandma loves me when we bake together
and she lets me pour, stir, mix, sift and measure—
smiling as I spill the flour, forget the baking powder
or stick my fingers into the dough.

I know my grandma loves me when we go to the beach
and the sun hasn't quite taken the chill out of the air,
the waves are crashing against the shore,
the wind is blowing sand in her face, and yet
she waits with open arms and a big, soft, fuzzy towel
to warm me up when I return shivering from the water.

I know my grandma loves me when the leaves turn red and yellow,

purple and brown and they fall to the ground,

leaving her with thousands of leaves to rake into piles,

and still with a grin she jumps in the leaves with me

and we throw them up UP UP into the air,

watching as they dance across the sky and over the grass

finally landing—

        scattered all over her yard.

I know my grandma loves me
when she looks at me
and her eyes light up
like stars twinkling in the night.